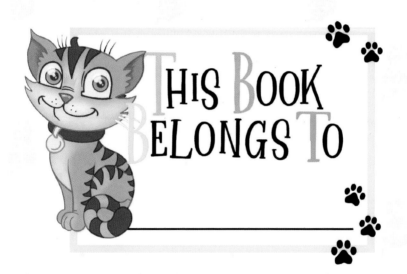

THIS BOOK
BELONGS TO

For information regarding press, media rights, foreign rights, licensing, promotions, and advertising
e-mail: marketing@dynamite.com

Cover Art by Ken Haeser
Book design by Cathleen Heard and Alexis Persson

Dynamite Entertainment
113 Gaither Dr., Ste. 205
Mt. Laurel, NJ 08054
dynamite.com

Nick Barrucci: CEO / Publisher
Juan Collado: President / COO
Brandon Dante Primavera: V.P. of IT and Operations

Joe Rybandt: Executive Editor
Matt Idelson: Senior Editor

Alexis Persson: Creative Director
Rachel Kilbury: Digital Multimedia Associate
Katie Hidalgo: Graphic Designer
Nick Pentz: Graphic Designer

Alan Payne: V.P. of Sales and Marketing
Vincent Faust: Marketing Coordinator

Jim Kuhoric: Vice President of Product Development
Jay Spence: Director of Product Development
Mariano Nicieza: Director of Research & Development

Print ISBN: 978-1-5241-2065-8
Hardcover ISBN: 978-1-5241-2095-5
Signed Hardcover ISBN: 978-1-5241-2096-2

First Printing
Printed in Korea

Names: Rybandt, Kristen, author. | Haeser, Ken, illustrator. | Rybandt, Joseph, editor.
Title: Saved By A Whisker / written by Kristen Rybandt ; illustrations by Ken Haeser; edited by Joseph Rybandt.
Description: Mt. Laurel, NJ: Dynamite Entertainment, 2021. | Summary: This is the story of how Cozmo - separated and left behind from his loving family - went on the journey of his life!
Identifiers: ISBN: 978-1-5241-2065-8 (paperback) | 978-1-5241-2066-5 (epub) | 978-1-5241-2067-2 (pdf)
Subjects: LCSH Cats--Juvenile fiction. | Family--Juvenile fiction. | CYAC Cats--Fiction. | Family--Fiction. | BISAC JUVENILE FICTION / Animals / Cats | JUVENILE FICTION / Action & Adventure / General
Classification: LCC PZ7.1 .R955 Sa 2021 | DDC [E]--dc23

SAVED
BY A
WHISKER

WRITTEN BY
KRISTEN RYBANDT

ILLUSTRATIONS BY
KEN HAESER

EDITED BY
JOSEPH RYBANDT

SPECIAL THANKS TO
PAMELA OTT

DYNAMITE®

Cozmo had a perfect view of Ella's room from inside the moving box. He could see through a small hole when she looked under the bed and even inside the dollhouse. Cozmo stayed perfectly still while Ella checked underneath her desk and behind the door. When she backed up against the side of the moving box, he sprung out like one of those surprise snakes in a can.

"Rowrr!" he yelled. Ella's eyes grew wide and her mouth formed a little "o" before she collapsed on the floor in giggles. She scratched Cozmo between his silver-gray ears just the way he liked. He purred in approval.

"You're such a good hider, buddy" she said. "This time I'll hide and you come find me, okay?"

Just then her mom called up the stairs. "The moving truck is here!"

Ella looked out the window and took off down the stairs in a thunder of footsteps. Cozmo jumped up on the bedside table to see what had gotten her so excited. He knew something was up because there were boxes everywhere.

Normally Cozmo loved boxes, but most of these were taped shut and no fun at all. He looked through the window and saw two large men carry his favorite green chair out of the house and disappear into the back of a big truck. He got a funny feeling in his belly and thought about going back into the box to hide when Ella's mom came into the room. She was carrying the red cage which usually meant a trip to the vet. Normally Cozmo would have gone to hide under the bed, but his red cage felt familiar and safe. He went in without a fight.

"It's okay, Cozmo," she said. "We're just going on a little car ride. You'll love our new place. It'll be summer all year long."

Cozmo soon realized there was nothing little about this car ride. It went on forever. Every time he dozed off, the car stopped or turned, and he slid against the side of the cage. He needed out. Why did they need to move to summer anyway? It was summer time right now. How could Ella sleep through all of this, he wondered.

"Meow," Cozmo said, quietly at first. Ella stirred and pet his little face through the squares of the cage, but soon fell back asleep.

"MEOWRRRR," he said again. Ella sat up again and opened the cage to let Cozmo out. It was dark outside, but he could tell they were moving very fast. He climbed unsteadily across her lap to get a better look out the window, but this only made his stomach feel worse.

Cozmo decided he probably shouldn't have eaten the entire bowl of kibble Ella had put inside his cage.

"MEOWRRRRRR!" cried Cozmo.

"Mom, I think something's wrong with Cozmo," Ella said.

"He probably just needs to use his litterbox," Ella's mom said. "We'll stop at the next rest area and take him out on his leash."

The car made several sharp turns and pulled into an almost empty parking lot. Ella's mom opened her door and a rush of warm, sticky air washed over the backseat. It smelled like wet dog.

Ella leaned over to snap the leash onto Cozmo's collar when a truck roared past. The engine snorted and rumbled. A vicious looking dog poked its snout through the truck's open window. It was so close, Cozmo could see drool hanging from the dog's chin.

"WOOF!" The dog's bark was deep and loud.

Cozmo locked eyes with Ella and gave her his help me look, but it was too late. Panic jolted through his body. He bucked away from her before she could finish snapping

the leash and launched himself out of the car through the open door. He took off across the parking lot towards the dark safety of a row of trees.

"Cozmo!" Ella yelled. She sounded scared too. He wondered if the dog had gotten loose and was chasing after him. He could hear it barking but couldn't tell how close it was. Cozmo's claws clicked against the hard pavement until he reached grass.

He dug into the soft ground and ran faster towards a path that looked too narrow for a big dog. He found a cluster of branches deep in the woods and huddled beneath it to catch his breath. His lungs ached and his heart pounded loudly in his ears.

The woods smelled wet and musky. He could still hear the dog barking, but at least it sounded far away. He heard people shouting and maybe calling his name, though it was hard to tell. After a long time, he heard more voices and loud sirens. Cozmo wondered what was happening back there, but he felt safe where he was. He wished Ella and her mom could hide with him. He curled into a tight ball and fell into a fitful sleep. 🐱

Cozmo woke from a terrible dream. In it he was being chased by a hulking, drooling creature. Every time he ran a different direction, the creature was there. It felt very real, but it must have been a dream because he could hear Ella calling his name. He blinked himself fully awake and remembered where he was. It was no dream.

He did hear someone, but it was not Ella. It sounded more like a cat. Cozmo poked his head out of the hollow of branches where he'd slept and found himself inches away from the most beautiful yellow eyes he'd ever seen. He'd never met a girl cat before. Actually, he couldn't remember

meeting any cat before. She had a fluffy coat of smoky gray fur. Cozmo couldn't stop staring.

"What's the matter?" she laughed. "Did you think you had the whole woods to yourself?"

"Uh no, I was just waiting to get back to my family and must have fallen asleep," he said. "Have you seen them?"

"Ohhh," she said. "You must be Cozmo."

"How'd you know?" he asked.

"Some lady and her kid were yelling for you all night. At one point they brought the entire fire department. Maybe they thought you got stuck in a tree or something. Anyway, they finally gave up around midnight and let us get some sleep. You look like you did alright."

"I can't believe I missed them," Cozmo said, looking behind the cat for any sign of his humans. All he could see were trees and more trees. "Did you see which way they went?"

"Nah, sorry. I'm Winnie, by the way. Why don't you come with me and meet the gang, and we'll see what's left for breakfast? You must be hungry."

Cozmo's stomach growled on cue. Underneath the hunger, his stomach felt cramped and cold. No way was he leaving the safety of the shelter he'd found.

"Maybe later. I might miss my family if they come looking for me."

"Suit yourself, but you might be here longer than you think," Winnie said.

Cozmo wondered what she meant by that. He'd never heard of a cat living in the woods. Had she lost her family? Before Cozmo got a chance to ask, he saw the tip of her tail swish behind a tree and then she was gone. 🐱

Cozmo stayed in the shelter all day. Even his stomach gave up on trying to get him out and stopped growling. He tried napping but there were strange sounds everywhere. The trees rustled and chirped above him. Things he couldn't see scurried through the brush around him. Cozmo was used to sounds of birds through the window or Ella's voice when she talked to him. The sounds in the woods were almost as scary as the vacuum cleaner. Even Winnie spooked him when she came back at dusk to check on him.

"Still here, huh?" she said.

"They didn't come back for me," Cozmo said.

"That's what I came to tell you. I think

they might still be around. My friend Jinx said he heard humans yelling for a cat a little while ago. It has to be you."

"You sure they were looking for me?" Cozmo asked.

"You're the only cat around here with a collar. A collar means you have a human. Come with me and we'll get you some grub and see if they come back."

The grub turned out to be a few scraps of kibble in a pie tin. Cozmo had never tasted anything so delicious in his life. A scruffy yellow cat missing half an ear gave Cozmo the hairy eyeball while he scarfed up what was left.

"Relax, Scratch," Winnie told him. "This is the cat those people have been looking for. He's temporary."

"Oh sure, Winn. Temporary. Right. Like you and me."

Cozmo was too hungry to care what Scratch meant by that. He decided the less he talked to or even looked at Scratch, the better. He glanced around at the trees and noticed a dozen set of eyes watching him from behind low branches. He should have felt less alone, but these eyes weren't exactly friendly.

"Did any of you guys see which way my people went?" Cozmo shouted in what was supposed to be his tough voice but sounded small and squeaky. The strange eyes blinked and stared back, but no one answered.

"I guess they aren't here anymore," Winnie said. "Why don't you stay here tonight and see if they come back."

Cozmo saw Scratch giving him the stink eye again and craved the comfort of his shelter from the night before.

"Nah, I'll check back in the morning. Night, Winnie."

"Be careful, Cozmo," she called out after him. 🐱

The next morning Cozmo woke to the sound of his stick shelter being pulled apart. Could it be Ella? He heard voices, but they were speaking cat.

"You sure this is the spot?" a low, deep voice said.

A pair of icy green eyes appeared inside the shelter. They belonged to a lanky black cat. Scratch stood behind him.

"You Cozmo?" asked the black cat.

"Who are you?" Cozmo asked.

"I'm Jinx and I think you know Scratch, but we don't have time for introductions. Follow me."

Cozmo followed without question. They walked along a maze of paths and jumped across a narrow stream. Cozmo thought about stopping to get a drink, but what Jinx wanted to show him felt more important.

"Look at what we found," said Jinx. They'd stopped at the edge of the woods. Cozmo saw the parking lot he'd run from last night. It was filled with cars, but he couldn't tell if one had his humans in it.

"I don't see them," he said to Jinx.

"Neither do we, but we do see you."

"Huh?"

"Look." Jinx pointed to a telephone pole by the edge of the parking lot. A bright pink piece of paper with Cozmo's picture splashed across the front was tacked to the side.

It read LOST CAT – CASH REWARD in bold black letters. There were numbers at the bottom and the word CALL WITH ANY INFO. Cozmo knew this had something to do with a phone and wished he had one. Also, fingers to work those tiny numbers on the screen.

"Wait, does this mean they're gone? What am I supposed to do?" Cozmo felt his throat squeeze up.

"I don't know what it means, but don't give up," said Jinx. "Pam might be able to help you."

"Who's Pam?"

"She's the lady who brings us food," Jinx said. "Didn't you wonder where it came from?"

"Not really. I always have food in my dish at home."

"Ha, of course. Well out here, my friend,

it's a little trickier," Jinx said. "We have to share our daily feast with each other and the possums and raccoons. Hey, everybody loves cat food. It's delicious!"

"What else do you eat then?" Cozmo asked.

"Lately we haven't had to worry about it. Pam and the rest of the gang are good to us," Jinx said.

"What happens if Pam doesn't feed us?" Cozmo asked.

"Let's not go there, little guy."

Jinx could tell this didn't exactly comfort Cozmo. "Have you ever fished before? Caught a mouse?"

"I got a catnip mouse at Christmas and Ella tells me I play a pretty mean game of fetch."

"Fetch?" Scratch howled. "What are you, some kind of dog?"

"Maybe we need to start thinking about Plan B," Jinx said.

"What's Plan B?" asked Cozmo.

Jinx looked at Cozmo and then at the lost cat sign. "But first, let's start with Plan M. It's time somebody taught you how to Mouse. Meet me back here when it gets dark."

"Don't fill up on catnip mice!" Scratch yelled, and Jinx elbowed him in his bony ribs. 🐱

Cozmo met Jinx back at the pie tin at dusk. It was hard to see Jinx with his all-black fur. Cozmo's silver stripes glowed in the dark. His stomach growled so loud Jinx looked up and grinned.

"See, this is why you need to learn to mouse. You're young and must be pretty fast to run that far away from your humans."

Cozmo followed Jinx along a faint trail through the woods. They passed another pie tin and water dish, and this one still had scraps in it.

"Why don't we just eat here?" he asked Jinx.

"Because that ain't ours. We don't take what don't belong to us."

Cozmo looked around and didn't see anyone else, but he could feel eyes following their every step.

They finally reached a small shed near the parking lot. Cozmo's stomach twisted up again. Jinx perched in front of a tiny dark hole towards the bottom of the shed. It was no bigger than a cat's paw. He looked over at Cozmo and nodded his head to show he should do the same. Cozmo sat and watched the hole. Nothing happened.

"What are we supposed to be doing?" Cozmo whispered.

"Shhhhhhhh," said Jinx. "They'll hear you. They have very good hearing."

"Who does?"

"The mice. Now, be quiet. I mean it. You'll never catch anything if it hears you coming."

Cozmo thought he saw a glint of tiny eyes just inside the dark hole, but then it was gone. He sat quietly next to Jinx until their eyelids drooped, and they both slipped into cat naps.

"Well look what we have here. A couple of ace mousers," Scratch chuckled behind them. Jinx jumped up and looked angrily at Cozmo like they'd both caught him napping.

"You know what, kid? You're on your own for awhile," Jinx said. "I got things to do, but you know what to do. Just sit here wait it out. They'll come out and, voilà, instant dinner."

Before Cozmo could ask questions, Jinx and Scratch were already gone. He didn't understand how sitting and staring at a hole would put food in his belly. He had tried staring at his food dish plenty of times at home, and that never worked. He kept watching the hole and felt his eyes start to droop again. Something skittered across his paw and he jerked it back. He looked down in horror and saw the tail of a tiny gray mouse trapped beneath his paw.

"Please don't eat me!" the mouse screamed. It bucked and strained to free its tail.

"I'm not going to eat you, but aren't you supposed to bring me food?" Cozmo lifted his paw and freed the mouse, who held his tail and looked at the cat in confusion.

"Huh? Bring you food?"

Cozmo looked at the mouse's tiny hands and realized he'd been the victim of a practical joke. Of course a mouse, especially one so tiny, could never carry more than a piece or two of kibble at a time. Jinx must have

thought he was pretty silly to fall for that one.

"Never mind. Just some cat's idea of a joke, I guess. Do you have any idea where a guy can get something to eat around here?"

"You're a cat. Why are you asking me for food?" the mouse said.

"I'm not getting much help from the other cats. They sent me over here to beg and that's what I'm doing," said Cozmo.

"Okay, well, hmm." The mouse scratched his chin with one paw and thought for a little bit. "I could draw you a map to all of the food dishes Pam fills up every day. Would that help?"

"Sure," said Cozmo.

"Okay, wait here. I'll be right back."

The mouse disappeared through the black

hole and came back with a nub of charcoal and a rolled-up leaf. He spread the leaf across the dirt and started drawing a map with the charcoal. The markings were tiny, but Cozmo recognized the shed and the woods. The mouse marked several Xs on the map. He explained those were places Pam and her helpers put fresh food and water every day for the cats.

"I only knew about one of those," Cozmo said, noticing another dish that was probably close to his shelter. "Why do you know where all the cat food is?"

"A mouse has to eat too. Cat food is delicious," he said. Cozmo's stomach growled in agreement.

"I'm Cozmo. What's your name?"

"Nice to meet you, Cozmo. I'm Tim." He

bowed with a flourish, holding the charcoal like a tiny baton.

Cozmo grinned. "I'm sorry for stepping on your tail."

"Oh, it didn't hurt. I just -- well, I never met a cat like you before, that's for sure."

Cozmo thanked Tim and picked the leaf up carefully in his mouth and carried it back to his shelter. He studied the map and decided to try the other locations to see if any food was left. He missed his food bowl at home, but more than that he missed Ella's ear scratches. He had to find something to eat and fresh water to drink or he wouldn't have the strength to find her again.

Cozmo followed the leaf map and found a pie tin filled with kibble just where Tim said it would be. He gobbled as much as his

belly would hold, half expecting Scratch or another cat to chase him off. He lapped up fresh water and wondered if any other cats knew about this place. Maybe he wouldn't mention it.

Cozmo noticed it was getting dark. He had never been out of his shelter at night. He ate a few more pieces of kibble and dragged his swollen belly back for the best sleep he'd had since getting lost. 🐱

Cozmo worked in a daily visit to Tim during his morning rounds. Every day he got up at dusk and swung by the secret feeding area. He soon realized it was not a complete secret. Some mornings the pie tin was brimming with kibble, but other times it was almost empty. The water was always fresh, especially after a good rain. Even when the kibble supply was low, Cozmo found a few pieces to take to Tim, who greeted him with a big grin.

"Cat food! My favorite! You're nothing like those other cats," Tim told Cozmo often.

Tim told Cozmo stories about Jinx's father, Lemmy, a lean brown tabby who used to stake out their mouse hole from sunup to sundown. He had managed to eat several of Tim's relatives, mostly second cousins twice removed. Cozmo's eyes widened in horror and then disgust when he thought about eating a mouse. Tim said the mice celebrated the day Lemmy suddenly stopped showing up to terrorize them. He said they thought Pam took Lemmy in, or maybe a coyote got him.

"Are there coyotes around here?" Cozmo asked, looking around nervously.

"Probably not. But there are some nasty raccoons. They hit that food dish you like so much. That's why most cats don't go there. Just make sure you go during the day because that's when raccoons sleep."

Cozmo was nodding when Jinx walked up and sat beside him. Tim had already vanished inside the mouse hole.

"Who're you talking to, Squirt?" Jinx asked.

"Oh, just myself," Cozmo said, his heart pounding.

"Is the mouse hole driving you batty? I know it does me sometimes. Thank goodness Pam feeds us," Jinx said.

"Have you ever met her? Pam?"

"Oh sure. I mean, I don't get close enough she can pet me or nothing, but I let her know I appreciate what she does for us. I give her the slow blink."

"What's that?" asked Cozmo.

"You know. It's when you look at someone and then close your eyes real slow and then open them again," said Jinx.

"Oh, you mean when you tell a human I love you," said Cozmo.

"Whatever you want to call it," Jinx said. "Most humans think purring is where it's at, but the real show of trust is when we give the slow blink."

Suddenly Cozmo found himself missing Ella very much.

"Hey Jinx, remember when you mentioned Plan B?" Cosmo asked. "Does it have anything to do with Pam?"

"No luck mousing, huh?" Jinx said and then eyed him suspiciously. "You look like you're getting something to eat. You've been out here, what, at least a month now."

"I'm just curious what Plan B is," Cozmo said quickly. "You seemed excited about it."

"Plan B," Jinx said thoughtfully. "I'll talk to Winnie and see what she thinks. I'll let you get back to your mousing."

Jinx was gone awhile before Tim poked his head out of the hole again.

"What's this about Plan B?" Tim asked.

"Mice must have better hearing than cats," Cozmo said. "I don't really know what Plan B is, only that Jinx thought I needed to learn to be a mouser first."

"You're definitely a good mouser in my book," Tim said, and they both laughed.

7

Winnie and Jinx came by Cozmo's shelter the next day to explain Plan B.

"So, you know how there's that flyer out there with your picture on it?" Jinx asked.

"Was out there, you mean," Cozmo said.

"Well yeah. I guess the rain pretty much ruined it, but Winnie memorized the number. She thought maybe we could try calling the number and turn you in for the cash reward."

"Really it's about getting you home, Cozmo," Winnie added.

"Wait, call the number? How?" Cozmo asked.

Cozmo remembered the time Ella's mom left her phone on the coffee table and he'd tried to order a pizza. He kept hitting the wrong numbers with his clumsy paws. He accidentally dialed a Chinese restaurant instead and was about to order the biggest feast of his life when Ella's mom took the phone away.

"I'm so sorry," she'd said to the person on the other end. "My cat accidentally called you. I cat-dialed you."

Cozmo didn't see Plan B working. Plus, there was the small matter that none of the cats had a phone.

"Leave that part to me," Jinx said with a smile.

A few days later, Jinx and Winnie visited

Cozmo at his shelter and told him the plan. Winnie scratched out the phone number with her paw in the dirt and told Cozmo to commit it to memory.

"Okay. Then what?" Cozmo asked.

"Then you follow us," Jinx said.

Cozmo stared at the numbers and repeated them over and over again. Winnie encouraged him while Jinx paced nervously.

Once Cozmo had the number memorized, Jinx led them along windy paths and underneath fallen branches until they came to a new edge of the woods and a cluster of houses. They walked along the sides of tall wooden fences that connected each yard and listened for dogs each time they came to a new one. Jinx stopped at one and led Winnie and Cozmo to the front and an open garage door.

"The phone's in there," he said, pointing his nose towards the garage.

The garage was set up like a workshop. Silver tools lined one wall with a workbench underneath. The place was as neat as a pin but Cozmo didn't see a phone.

"Where is it?" he asked Jinx.

"It's there, hanging right by the door to the house," Jinx said.

Cozmo was sure Jinx was playing another joke on him. The only thing he saw by the door was a small black box with a loopy wire hanging from it.

"You think that's a phone?" asked Cozmo, puzzled.

"Yes, yes," Jinx said. "It's a phone. Kids." He rolled his eyes.

"It's got number buttons and I'm thinking

if you jump up on the table and knock the handle part off, you can push the numbers with your nose, see?" Jinx explained.

Cozmo only saw how high up the phone was on the wall and how far away the workbench was from the phone.

"Wait. I have to jump up there? I can't do that. What if someone comes?"

"If they see you, maybe they'll call animal control and you'll find your humans even sooner. Don't you have one of them chips humans use to find lost cats?"

"I don't know. I don't think so." Cozmo didn't like the sound of animal control.

"Anyway, what if I fall?" Cozmo said.

"You're a cat," said Jinx. "You have nine lives."

"If it's no big deal, why don't you do it?" Cozmo asked.

"I'm afraid of heights, okay?" Jinx said. Cozmo couldn't imagine Jinx being afraid of anything.

"Why don't we try it another time, guys." Winnie said. "I bet we can get Scratch to jump up there." Something about the mention of Scratch made Cozmo sit up tall.

"I'll do it," Cozmo said.

"Are you sure?" Winnie and Jinx asked at the same time.

Cozmo crept across the cold cement floor of the garage. He stayed low to the ground and listened for any sounds coming from the house. He tried not to think about how nervous he felt.

He moved to the edge of the workbench and did some quick math in his head to figure out how far he'd need to jump. He landed on the surface with ease. Reaching the phone was going to be trickier. He could knock the handle part off, no problem, but how was he going to push the number buttons? The black box looked too narrow to land on and there wasn't much to hold onto. Good thing Ella's mom never had him declawed.

He did some more mental math and wiggled his hind legs to line up the jump. He flew through the air gracefully and landed against the phone at a perfect angle. The handle part sprung loose from the cradle and rattled noisily to the ground. Cozmo knew he had to act fast, so he leapt up to the workbench and lined up a jump to the phone again. He wasn't sure how he was going to hold on, but it was now or never.

The door to the house suddenly flew open and a man in a white undershirt and pajama

pants stared at the phone on the floor and Cozmo on his workbench in stunned surprise.

Cozmo froze, unable to think, let alone move a muscle. The man looked more surprised than angry.

"What's going on in here?!"

Winnie and Jinx both whisper-yelled at Cozmo from outside the garage, "RUN!!"

Cozmo's brain connected with his muscles, and he clicked into high gear, bounding down from the table and out of the garage as fast as he could. Winnie and Jinx were right behind him. They didn't stop until they were safe in the woods again.

The three cats huddled and tried to catch their breath beneath an old oak tree that was already as familiar to Cozmo as Ella's room used to be.

"So much for Plan B," Jinx said and started laughing. Soon Winnie joined in. Neither could seem to stop. Cozmo didn't see what was so funny about him almost getting caught by a human, but Winnie's laughter was contagious, and he couldn't help himself. Soon they were all breathless again from laughter. Cozmo felt the fear drift away.

"How long have you been lost, Jinx?" Cozmo asked.

"Not all of us are lost, kid. I actually grew up out here. Born and raised. My dad was one of the founding fathers of our colony of strays," Jinx said.

"Oh," said Cozmo, pretending he didn't already know about Lemmy. Cozmo was now used to cats living in the woods, but he hadn't thought about them being born there.

"What about you, Winnie?" Cozmo asked.

"Oh, I've been here since I was just a kitten," she said gently.

"What happened to your family?" Cozmo asked.

"I don't remember them. I'll never know why they left me, but I sure am glad I found Jinx and the gang. They're my family now," Winnie said.

"You at least have a chance to find your humans again," Jinx told Cosmo. "I think it's time for Plan C."

"Plan C?" Cozmo gulped. Plan M had worked out okay, but only because he did the opposite of what Jinx had in mind. Plan B had almost been a disaster.

"Plan C is we get Pam to help us," Winnie said.

Even though Cozmo still had never met or even seen Pam yet, this didn't seem like a bad idea at all. 🐱

8

Pam and her crew visited the woods every morning without fail. They came when it rained, and Winnie and Jinx said they even came when it snowed. The leaves had changed colors on the trees and the nights were already cold. Cozmo didn't want to think about sleeping in the snow.

"If you sit right here, you'll have a good view," Winnie told Cozmo, guiding him to a spot inside a shelter made up of old wooden crates. Cozmo had never been allowed this far into the big cat shelter before. He could see Scratch glaring at him like he didn't belong. Cozmo pretended not to notice.

At ten o'clock on the dot, a woman with long dark hair arrived with two other women trailing behind. Their arms were filled with bags of kibble and jugs of water.

"The one with the long hair is Pam," said Winnie.

Cozmo noticed the rest of the cats stayed hidden and quiet while Pam and the other women refilled the food and water supply. Once the humans backed off, several cats crept over to get a bite to eat. Cozmo figured it was safe to join in and walked to an opening next to Scratch.

"What do you think you're doing, pal?" Scratch spat. The fur on his back stood up in spikes and his ears were leaned back.

"I-I-I just thought--" Cozmo started.

"Get BACK!" Scratch ordered.

Cozmo slunk back towards the crates.

"Wait up, little guy," a soft voice called out. It was Pam.

Cozmo stopped in his tracks and looked back at her. Pam had crouched down and was holding her hand out to him.

"I haven't seen you around here before. Are you new?" she asked.

Cozmo was tired of being scared all the time. His body ached from hunger and a cough he couldn't seem to shake. Something about the sweetness in her voice reminded him of Ella. He turned and walked towards her.

"Where are you going, moron?" Scratch called out.

"Thatta boy, Coz," Winnie said, still inside the crate shelter.

Pam stayed crouched down while Cozmo

approached her cautiously. He rubbed his head against her knee and she scratched gently between his ears. He purred and went back for more pets, meeting her hand with his head each time.

"Aren't you a little lovebug?" Pam said. She felt the collar around his neck, and read his gold tag. "Cozmo, huh. I don't see a phone number, but something tells me you aren't a stray."

After a satisfying round of chin and ear scratches, Pam stood up and walked back to the other women. Cozmo could see them talking but couldn't hear what they said. Pam disappeared, and his heart sank. He looked around at the other cats, some still waiting by the sidelines for the bigger cats, like Scratch, to finish eating. Cozmo thought about sneaking off to the secret dish but doubted it would be filled yet if the humans were still here. He was so very tired and hungry.

Pam reappeared carrying something familiar. It looked like Cozmo's red carrier, except this one was blue. She walked up to Cozmo and pet him some more before picking him up. He let her put him inside the carrier without a fight, even though his heart was pounding.

What was happening, he wondered? Was she going to take him to his family or some-where worse than the woods? The door to the carrier snapped shut and Cozmo felt himself being carried through the woods to the parking lot where he'd gotten lost a million years ago. Pam opened a car door and put the carrier on the back seat.

"First, we're going to make a stop and get

you checked out," she told Cozmo. "I don't like the sound of that cough."

The movement of the car and safety of the carrier made him feel so tired, he couldn't keep his eyes open a moment longer. He curled against the side of the carrier and dozed the rest of the car ride. 🐱

9

"Let's get a look at this guy," a woman wearing a white coat said.

Pam set the carrier on the metal table and opened the door. Cozmo slowly stepped out. It looked kind of like his vet's office back home and definitely smelled like it. The woman gently looked inside his ears, squeezed around his belly, and listened to his back with one of those funny looking things vets plug into their ears.

"He's definitely got a little cold, but nothing some medicine won't fix," the vet told Pam.

She gave Cozmo something terrible to drink, followed by a dish of delicious wet food. Cozmo lapped it up but was happy when

it was time to climb back inside the carrier. Pam took him back to her car and drove him a short distance to a big house.

They went inside, and Pam set the carrier down inside a small room and let him out. He nosed around and was relieved to find they were alone. Pam left the room and came back with a bowl of food and some water. She made a bed for Cozmo out of some soft blankets in a corner of the room. He noticed a litterbox in another corner. He hadn't used one of those in awhile but remembered how it worked.

"I know you must belong to someone," she said to Cozmo. "I'm going to do some asking around, but for now you can stay here." She left him to catch up on some long overdue cat naps. 🐱

10

Cozmo woke to the delicious smell of roast turkey. His stomach growled so he walked over to the bowl of kibble in Pam's kitchen. The day before she'd taken him back to the vet, who gave him a clean bill of health. Now he could roam with the rest of the cats at Pam's house. He hadn't met them all, but the ones he had met were more like Winnie and Jinx than Scratch. Cozmo felt sad thinking about Winnie, Jinx, and Tim. They would probably all love it here, he thought.

A chatty Siamese named Spatz filled Cozmo in. He explained that a few of the cats lived with Pam, but the rest were waiting for their forever homes.

"Are any of them lost, like me?" asked Cozmo.

"Maybe at some point," Spatz said. "I was lost, but that was years ago so I don't really think of it that way anymore. I got a family coming to look at me soon. Pam's been making me pose for pictures while I'm trying to nap so she can show them how cute I am. I'm like, can't you see I'm napping over here? These humans with their phones, am I right?"

Cozmo smiled and nodded. Pam had been taking lots of pictures of him too. "Do you happen to have a cat here named Lemmy?" he asked Spatz.

"Oh sure," Spatz said. "Who could forget Lemmy. What a charmer. Nearly took my head off for sleeping in his spot once."

"Is he still here?" Cozmo looked around nervously.

"Don't worry. He got adopted. Gloated about it nonstop until the family came to get him. They had three little kids all ready to pet the nice kitty," Spatz chuckled.

"Adopted," Cozmo said. He wished he could tell Jinx.

"From what I hear, you may not need to wait like the rest of us," Spatz said.

"What do you mean?" Cozmo asked.

Spatz looked around, then spoke in a lower voice. "You didn't hear it from me, but you're getting a visitor from Florida tomorrow."

"Florida?" said Cozmo. "Where's that? I don't know anyone in Florida."

"Like I said, you didn't hear it from me," Spatz said. "Get some rest today. You'll wanna lay low anyway because it's Thanksgiving and that means this place is gonna be overrun with humans in a couple of hours."

Cozmo took Spatz' advice and stayed in his room and out of the way. The smell of good food drifted in, along with the sounds of happy humans. Their voices and laughter were both strange and comforting. He had just drifted off into another catnap when Pam appeared beside him.

"I've got a surprise for you, buddy," Pam said. She held some shredded turkey in the palm of her hand. Cozmo took small bites and purred in appreciation. The house was quiet again and it was dark outside. He was glad to be inside where it was warm and he didn't have to worry about rain or snow. Cozmo gave Pam the slow blink and drifted off to sleep again, still purring.

The next morning Cozmo awoke to the smell of bacon and voices in the other room. They were high pitched and excited. Cozmo wondered if Spatz' forever home came through and if his friend was about to get a new human sister or three.

Pam appeared in the doorway with a woman just behind her. Then a smaller person rushed past them both to the blankets where Cozmo was still curled up.

"COZMO!" the girl cried.

He knew that voice anywhere. It was Ella!

Cozmo felt himself swept into her arms. She smothered his head with kisses and he returned the favor with his own enthusiastic head kisses.

"I can't believe it's really you," Ella said.

Ella's mom joined them, smiling.

"I'm so glad I gave a flyer to Mr. Hoopes," Ella's mom told Pam.

"I know," said Pam. "He's always been good to the strays. He told me he once found a cat in his garage trying to make a phone call. He thinks it was one of the strays trying to call me," she laughed.

"I'm so glad you paid him a visit," Ella's mom said. "If you hadn't, we might never have found Cozmo."

Ella and her mom were petting a deeply contented looking Cozmo. "Mom, can we bring him home now?" Ella asked.

"We sure can," her mom said. "Let's get him in the carrier and then we should get going to the airport."

Ella looked at her mom and said, "But

no stopping and absolutely no leash this time." They both looked at Cozmo and laughed. It was music to his ears.

ABOUT SAVED WHISKERS

SavedWhiskers Rescue Organization, Inc. (SWRO) was founded by Pamela J. Ott, a certified veterinary technician, and was incorporated May 6, 2003 as a 501(c)3 non-profit cat and kitten rescue.

SWRO is dedicated to saving the lives of countless felines by rescuing abused, abandoned and homeless cats, providing veterinary care and shelter until they can be placed into a loving home. We are a volunteer organization which relies solely on monetary donations. All funds go directly toward the care of the cats we rescue.

"Whiskers" (the cat pictured in their logo above) was the cat that started it all. He was rescued back on January 17, 2003 from an abusive owner and eventually rehabilitated for a new loving home.

Vistt them at: http://www.savedwhiskersrescue.com/
and https://www.facebook.com/SavedWhiskersRescue/

THE AUTHOR

Kristen Rybandt lives in West Chester, Pennsylvania with her husband, two daughters, and two spoiled house cats. In her spare time, she loves to write and volunteer with cats from a local rescue, while posting too many photos on instagram because she hopes seen equals saved and also because cats are really cute. She first learned about the amazing work Saved Whiskers does almost two decades ago and has been a fan ever since.

THE ARTIST

Ken Haeser is a comic book artist and writer, and graduate of the Joe Kubert School of comic art. He is best known for his work on the Grumpy Cat graphic novel by Dynamite Entertainment and covers for comics like Batman/TMNT, Back to the Future, and Flash Gordon.

You Can Make a Difference!

If you've ever adopted a cat, or any animal, from a shelter or rescue organization, you saved it from a much harder life as a stray. You gave it the comfort of a warm place to sleep, a full belly, and good medical care. You loved it and treated it like a member of the family. Which it is!

Still, not all homeless cats are ready to be adopted as pets. Some may be too scared of people or used to living on their own. Have you ever seen a cat with a tip of their ear missing? It might look like they've been in a fight, but this is called ear-tipping and it means this cat has been spayed or neutered and released, which is a good thing. He or she probably also got its shots and a checkup. This helps keep the cats safe until they are ready for adoption.

One way you can help a homeless pet become a member of someone else's family is by volunteering at your local animal shelter or rescue organization. Many places allow kids to volunteer with a parent or guardian. You might be able to help with tasks like filling up food and water bowls or playing with the cats. This is called socialization and gets them more used to being around people, which gives them a better chance of being adopted. Plus you get to play with cats. It's a win-win.

Some families even volunteer to foster a cat until it's ready to be adopted. This is a big commitment since the cat or kitten comes to live with you temporarily. But it can also be extremely rewarding to know you helped prepare a cat for its forever home.

The next time you have a birthday party, consider asking for donations of pet food and supplies instead of gifts. Imagine how great it will feel to deliver a big box of supplies and treats to the cute pups and cats waiting for homes at your local animal rescue. Places that help feed and care for homeless animals never have too many supplies.

If you already have a cat or kitten at home, you know how much they love to play. Many shelters take donations of DIY cat toys. Cat wands, catnip sachets, and no-sew fleece blankets are just a few crafts you could make with a little help.

There is a steady supply of good people who help make sure homeless cats are fed and cared for as much as possible. There is an even bigger supply of new cats and kittens needing that care, so every chance you get to help a cat in need makes a big difference! 🐱